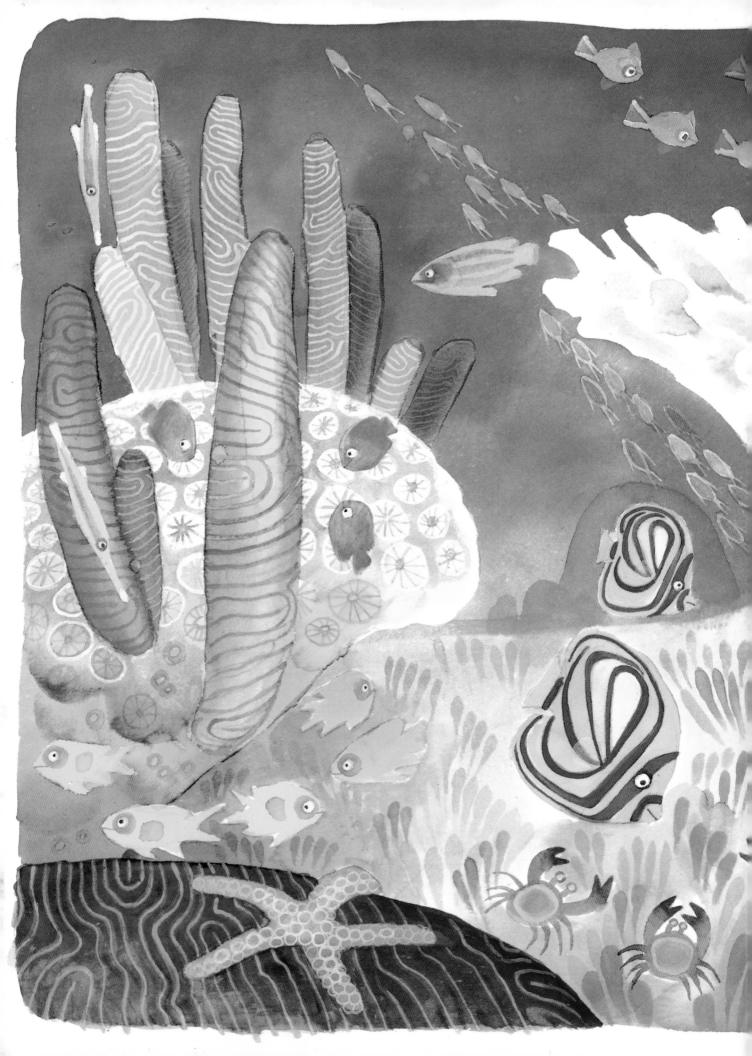

MYRIAD BOOKS LIMITED
35 Bishopsthorpe Road, London SE26 4PA

First published in 1990 by
FRANCES LINCOLN LIMITED
4 Torriano Mews, Torriano Avenue
London NW5 2RZ

ISBN 1 84746 052 6
EAN 9 781 84746 052 3

Printed in China

CURIOUS CLOWNFISH

ADRIENNE KENNAWAY
STORY BY ERIC MADDERN

MYRIAD BOOKS LIMITED

In the warm waters of the coral reef swam many fabulous fish.

But one fish always stayed at home and never even went out to play. This was timid Clownfish, who spent all day in the waving arms of Anemone. Nibbling food, she kept Anemone clean, and the stinging tentacles protected her from danger.

So it went on for a long time, until. . .

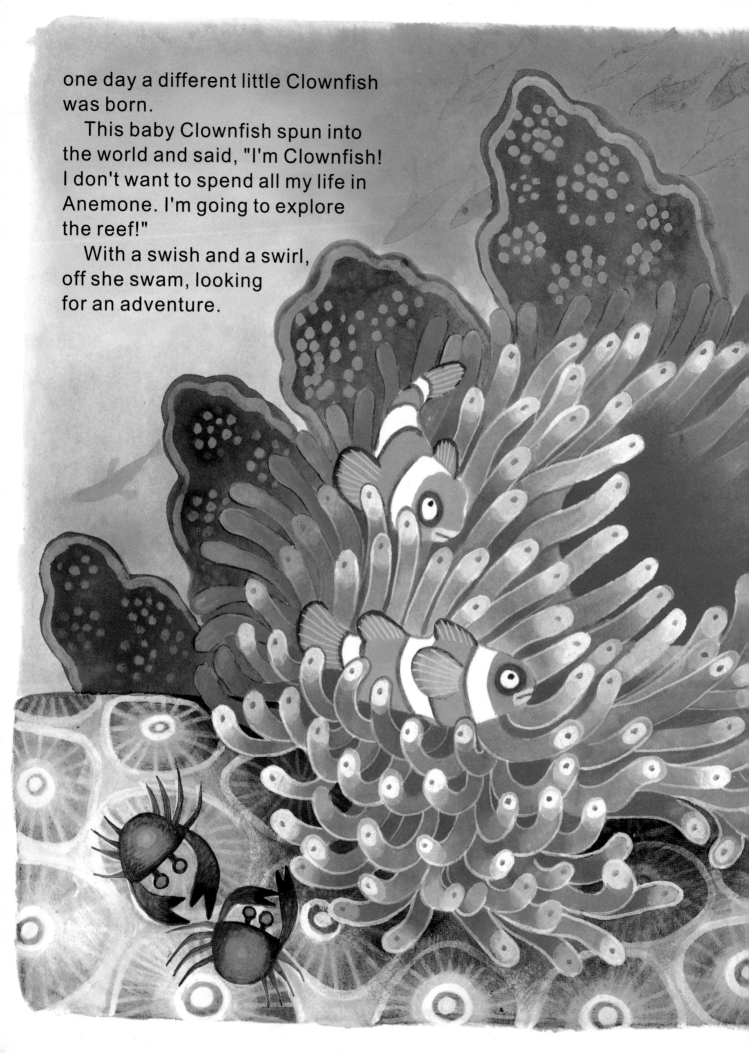

one day a different little Clownfish
was born.
    This baby Clownfish spun into
the world and said, "I'm Clownfish!
I don't want to spend all my life in
Anemone. I'm going to explore
the reef!"
    With a swish and a swirl,
off she swam, looking
for an adventure.

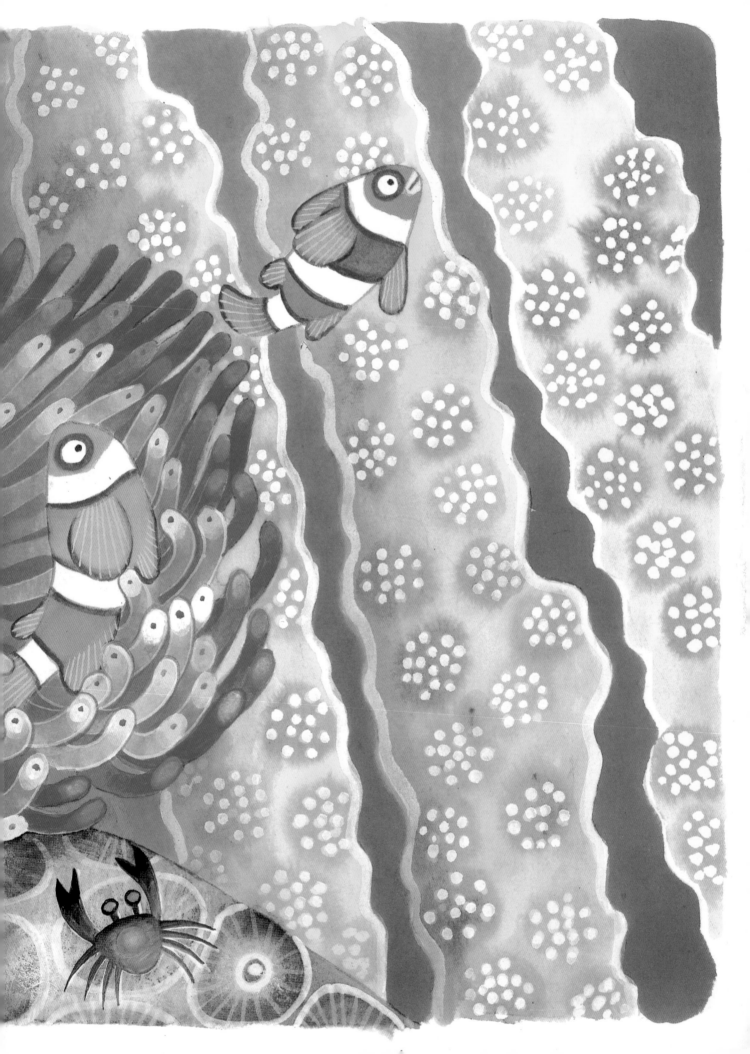

She frisked through the pool, past blue Sea Star, past fans and fingers of coral.
Then suddenly she saw slinky Sea Slug, waving and dancing through the water. "I'd love to dance like that," she thought, and swam up close to join in.
But the water near Sea Slug tasted horrible, so Clownfish quickly swam off again.

Next Clownfish saw a huge spiky fish crunching on the coral.

"Poor thing, he looks sad," she thought. "I'll cheer him up." And she swam close to give him a clean.

But old Porcupine Fish must have frightened himself, because he puffed up like a big prickly ball.

"Whoops!" said Clownfish, and stopped just in time. She didn't want prickly lips.

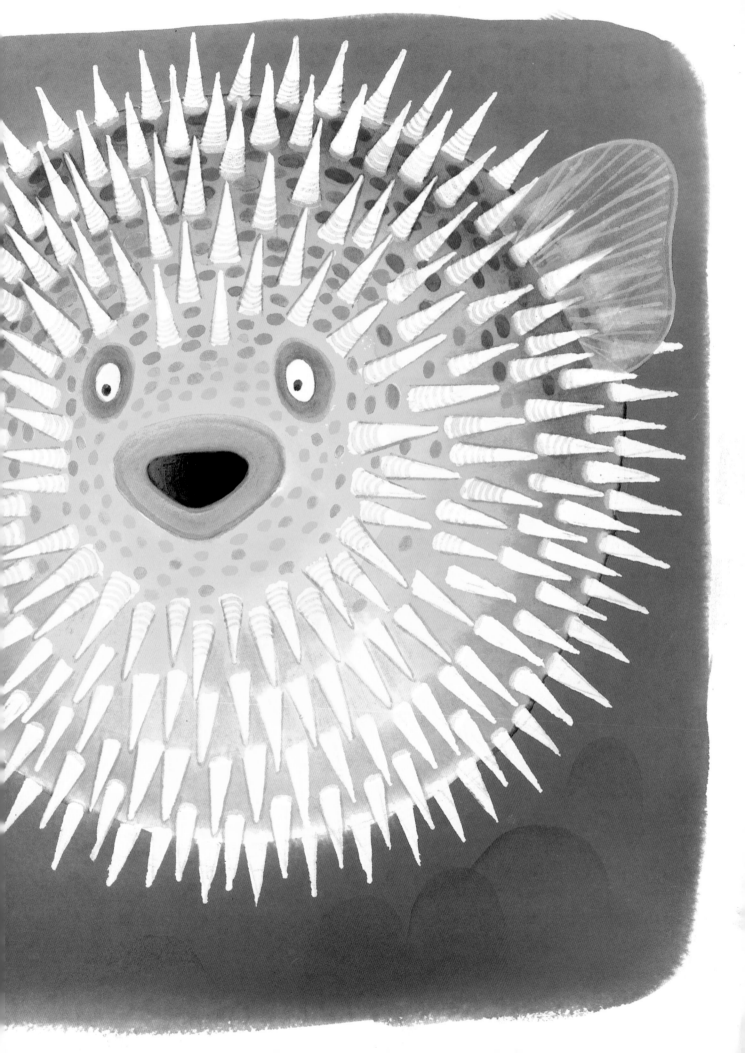

"Isn't anyone friendly?" Clownfish was wondering,
when Spottyfish sailed by with her babies.
   "Ah!" thought Clownfish, "can I come too?"
And she tagged along, playing with the little ones.
   Just as she was thinking "This is fun!" Spottyfish hurried them into the coral. When Clownfish
looked to see the trouble, she saw . . .

fiery Dragonfish!

Gliding along with her long spines
waving, she was quite a pretty sight.
But the little fish were all dashing to
hide, and soon Clownfish saw why.

One poor fish was stung by a spine
and instantly rolled over dead.
Dragonfish gobbled him up in one
mouthful and floated on by.

Clownfish was frightened by Dragonfish and knew she had to take care. She left Spottyfish and swam around looking for a place to rest.

A big empty shell looked all right, and she was just about to swim in when out shot the claws of crabby old Crab.

Clownfish escaped with a scratch on her tail.

Spiralling slowly through the water
Clownfish came upon Sweetlips.
    She could hardly believe her eyes,
for dancing in and out of his mouth
were two little Blue-Streaked Cleaners,
keeping Sweetlips clean.
    "That's what I do for Anemone!"
She cried. "Please, please can I help?"

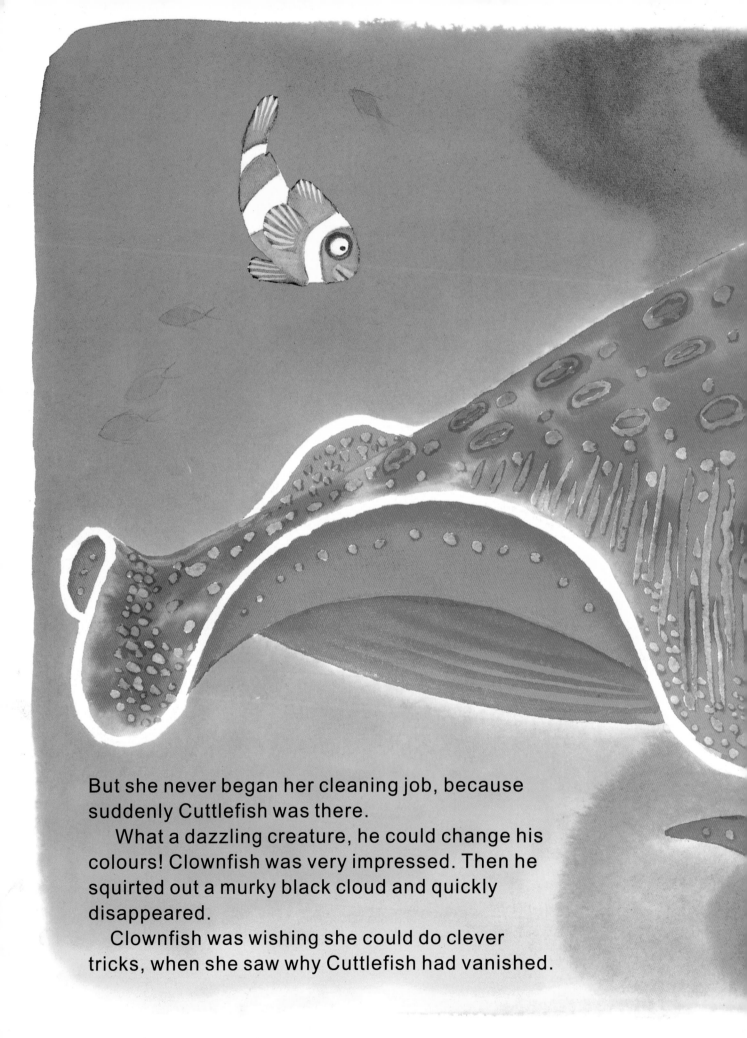

But she never began her cleaning job, because
suddenly Cuttlefish was there.

　What a dazzling creature, he could change his
colours! Clownfish was very impressed. Then he
squirted out a murky black cloud and quickly
disappeared.

　Clownfish was wishing she could do clever
tricks, when she saw why Cuttlefish had vanished.

Through the black cloud the face of Eel came snapping, and Clownfish's heart skipped a beat. Eel was looking right at her. She knew it was time to go.

She turned and swam but was so scared she didn't know how to go straight. Twisting, frisking, looping and drooping, she made the Eel confused. But slowly, slowly his snapping jaws came closer, closer and closer.

Then Clownfish saw the most welcome sight she'd seen for a long, long while.

It was a ring of waving tentacles. Anemone at last. In she slipped just in time and Eel got stung on the nose!

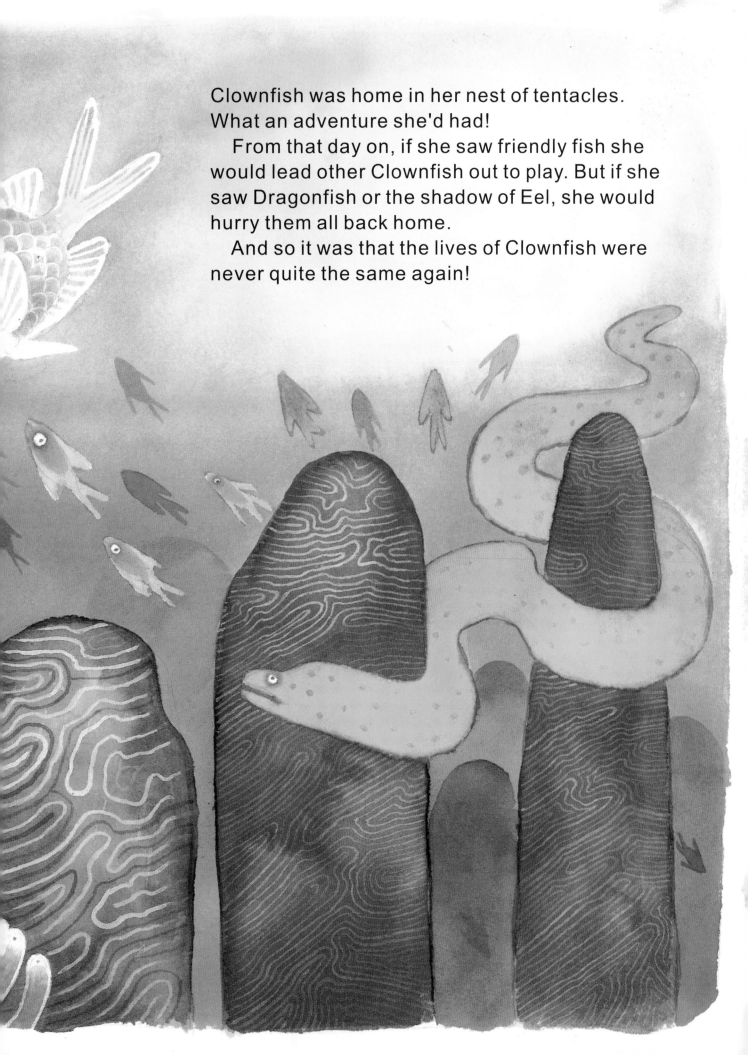

Clownfish was home in her nest of tentacles.
What an adventure she'd had!

From that day on, if she saw friendly fish she
would lead other Clownfish out to play. But if she
saw Dragonfish or the shadow of Eel, she would
hurry them all back home.

And so it was that the lives of Clownfish were
never quite the same again!

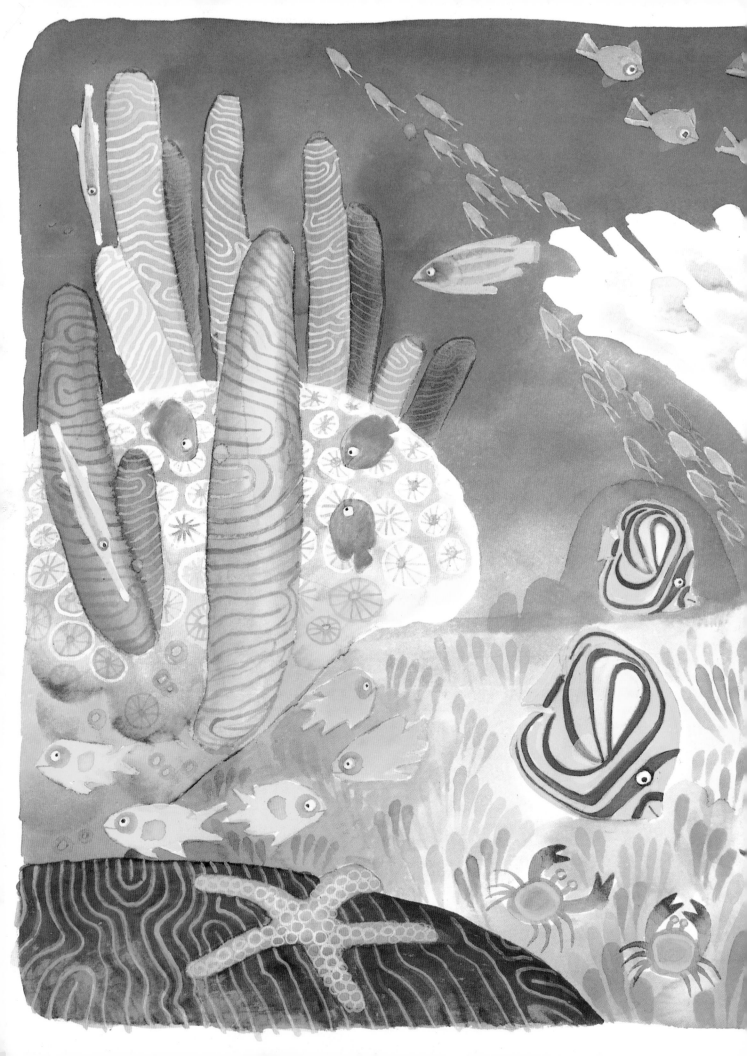